A Sudden Drop

Ali Sparkes

Illustrated by
Simon Bartram

OXFORD
UNIVERSITY PRESS

OXFORD
UNIVERSITY PRESS

Great Clarendon Street, Oxford, OX2 6DP,
United Kingdom

Oxford University Press is a department of the University of Oxford.
It furthers the University's objective of excellence in research, scholarship,
and education by publishing worldwide. Oxford is a registered trade mark of
Oxford University Press in the UK and in certain other countries

Text © Ali Sparkes 2017

Illustrations © Simon Bartram 2017

The moral rights of the author have been asserted

First published 2017

British Library Cataloguing in Publication Data
Data available

978-0-19-837759-7

1 3 5 7 9 10 8 6 4 2

Paper used in the production of this book is a natural, recyclable product
made from wood grown in sustainable forests. The manufacturing process
conforms to the environmental regulations of the country of origin.

Printed in China by Leo Paper Products Ltd.

Acknowledgements
Inside cover notes written by Karra McFarlane

Contents

Chapter 1
The Pits

Bella was minding her own business when she fell through the pavement.

She was on her way to school, just walking past Moody's News, when the ground under her feet crumbled away to nothing. One second there were ordinary, solid, grey slabs and the next – nothing.

She didn't even have time to scream.

Beneath the pavement it was dark and cold and there were snakes. Red serpents writhed below her and a cascade of shiny grey beetles tumbled across her school jumper. Bella sucked in some air and bawled for help.

Mr Moody came out of his shop, reached down and hauled her up again. Together they stood, staring down into the snake pit. It was as deep as Bella was tall – and nearly as wide.

"Could've been worse," said Mr Moody, dusting some woodlice off Bella's shoulder. "Those old cables probably stopped you falling through to the bowels of the earth."

Bella stared down the hole, still shaking. Ah. Rusty iron cables. Not snakes.

"Cheer up, Bella!" said Mr Moody, with a laugh. "Don't worry – you're still in one piece!"

"But …" croaked Bella. "This doesn't happen *here*! Not in *Granford*! Nobody expects to drop through the pavement in Granford!"

Mr Moody scratched his bald head. "Is there anywhere people *do* expect to drop through the pavement?" he asked.

"I don't know," said Bella, biting the end of one of her dark plaits. Her voice was squeaky. "In countries where they have earthquakes and volcanoes, maybe. But not in Granford!"

"Go on," said Mr Moody. "You get to school and I'll phone the council."

Bella walked on. Her legs were grazed and shaky. When she told Sam about the hole at breaktime, he didn't believe her.

"Oh come off it," he said, flicking bits of screwed up paper at her head. "You just fell off the kerb. You never look where you're going."

"It was a hole!" protested Bella. But Sam didn't believe her until they were on their way home and he saw the hole for himself.

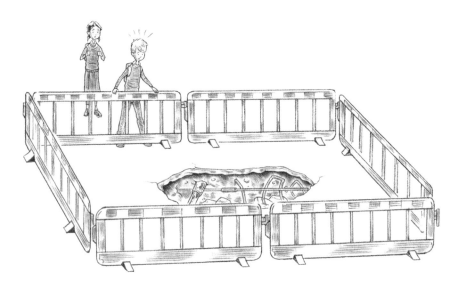

It was surrounded by bright orange safety barriers and was outside Moody's News, just as Bella had said.

"Wow," he said, his floppy red hair dangling over his forehead as he peered down into it. "There really *is* a hole."

The hole was on the TV news that night too. And it wasn't the only one. In the town's shopping centre an even bigger hole had opened up. An entire car had dropped into it. The driver and his elderly mother had to be rescued by firefighters.

"It seems," said the reporter, "that Granford really is the pits!"

Dad switched off the TV and sighed.

"Yeah, thanks," he muttered. "Great joke. Like we hadn't noticed."

He peered out of the window at the old brick factory which loomed on the horizon. Half the town had worked there once but it had closed down a year ago. Nobody worked there any more, so nobody walked past Top Trims – Mum and Dad's hair salon – on the way to their jobs. Every day Dad had fewer and fewer heads of hair to cut. Mum hadn't picked up her scissors for weeks.

Developers had bought the factory to turn into flats and then decided not to bother. Nobody left in Granford could afford to buy them.

"Well, at least you only fell down a *little* hole," said Mum, putting antiseptic on Bella's grazes. "It could have been worse."

The next day, it was worse.

Chapter 2
A Sinking Feeling

There was a sports field with a children's play area on the way to Agora Primary School. Normally Bella would meet Sam as he trekked over from his house on the other side of the field. Today she saw he was already there – but he wasn't on the swings as usual.

No. Today he was standing in the middle of the field, staring at the grass.

"Sam!" yelled Bella. "What are you *doing*?"

"Come over here!" he yelled back.

She ran across the field, her lunchbox thumping up and down in her backpack. "What? We're going to be late," she huffed.

Sam was still looking at the grass. Correction: he was looking at what *used* to be grass. Now it was nothing. Just empty space above a yawning dark hole.

Bella felt a chill run through her.
Another hole. It was about three metres
deep and oval in shape: big enough to
chuck a couple of bikes into. A punctured
football floated on a puddle of water
glittering at the bottom of it.

"That's five holes in one week," said Sam. "I looked it up online. The hole which the car went into, two smaller holes over in Basilica Road, the hole you fell in yesterday – and now this one."

He raised his eyes to Bella's and she could see he was a bit shaken up too. "What's *happening* to Granford? It's like a weird dream."

Bella nodded, gulping. "Maybe the whole town's going to slide into a big pit," she mumbled, remembering the news report on the TV. "Maybe everyone will have to move away."

"My mum said everyone's moving away anyway," said Sam. "There's no work here. The corner shop near us has closed. It's all boarded up."

"HEY! You two! Move AWAY from there!"

They looked up to see two men running across the field, carrying a bright orange safety barrier and a reel of wire.

"Go on! Get off to school!" panted one,
as they got closer. "That's dangerous. We're
here to block it off from kids like you."

"We're not stupid," said Bella. "We weren't going to jump into it!"

But they left the men to their work and walked on to school. Bella hoped their teacher, Mr Murphy, would still be there when they arrived. Three teachers had left this term and last week Mr Murphy had told them all this might be his last term too.

The classes were getting smaller and smaller and now Year 6 was being taught in with Year 5 – and there were still only eighteen of them put together. Agora Primary had always been a small school but now it was shrinking to a tiny school.

"You never know," said Sam. "Maybe there won't be any school today. There might just be a great big hole with some Year 1s swimming around in a puddle in the middle of it."

They both laughed but it wasn't good laughter. The bottom really *was* falling out of their world.

Chapter 3
Invisible People

Mr Murphy was still there, but two more children had left the school. There were holes in the ground where the earth had been and empty spaces in the classrooms where children had been, thought Bella. What would disappear next?

Mr Murphy loved history. It was his favourite subject and today he was talking about the Romans.

"I want you all to imagine a world without sewers," he said, peering at them with shining dark eyes.

"Think about it! What would it be like, living in Granford with no underground pipes to take away all the smelly stuff?"

The class groaned with disgust.

"It would be a stinky place," said Mr Murphy, grinning. "No sinks or baths or showers. Imagine that! You wouldn't want to go outside for a picnic, either – you'd be hit by swarms of flies and maybe catch a nasty disease like cholera!"

The class investigated how underground pipes worked. There were pipes taking away waste water.

And there were stacks of tiles under the floors: a fire heated the air between the tiles, which heated the rooms above. It was amazing to think that people who had lived centuries ago had invented it all, thought Bella. And they had to do it all with pottery because there was no such thing as plastic back then.

"And this is why we should love the Romans!" said Mr Murphy, at the end of the lesson. "Because they came to this country and built our first sewer systems. And bath houses. We owe a lot to the Romans."

Bella felt a bit more cheerful after the history lesson. She went to tell Mr Murphy about the hole she'd fallen into yesterday – and the one she and Sam had found in the park that morning.

"I've heard about these," said Mr Murphy. "They're called sinkholes."

"Sinkholes?" said Bella. "Because the ground just sinks?"

"That's right," said Mr Murphy. He tapped a few keys on his school laptop and some pictures came up: lots of different sinkholes around the world.

"See? Most are quite small, like the one you fell in – but some have been known to open up 600 metres wide and just as deep. Sinkholes are quite rare but we've been getting more of them around here recently because of our chalky soil."

"What's wrong with chalky soil?" Bella asked.

"Chalk dissolves when there's a lot of rain," said Mr Murphy. "Sometimes, underneath all the trees and grass and roots and soil, the chalk dissolves away and

there's a kind of hidden cavern left where it used to be. And then the top bit – the ground we walk on – can fall in without warning."

Bella gulped. "So – this whole school could just drop through the ground at any time?"

Her teacher laughed. "I hope not! This school is built on good, solid foundations," he said. "We'll be fine. Don't worry. You're more likely to win the lottery than fall in another sinkhole!"

"I wish Mr Murphy could stay," Bella said to Sam as they walked home. "We'll only have three teachers left once he goes. That's not enough!"

Sam looked down at his scuffed shoes. "My mum thinks the school will have to close," he said. "We'll have to go on the bus to the junior school in Clayesbourne. If we stay."

Bella stopped under the oak trees on the edge of the Minerva Woods. "What do you mean 'if we stay'? You're not *going?* Are you?"

Sam shrugged and looked away from her. "My dad's been offered a job at a big bakery. It's a *two hour* drive to get there. If he takes it, we'll have shut up Tasty Bakes and move away."

"But … you live *here*," was all Bella could think of to say.

"I *know* I live here!" snapped Sam. "But if there's nobody here to buy Dad's cakes and bread, then there's no money coming in and we can't afford to stay here."

"But …" Bella began.

"Look! Don't you get it?" yelled Sam. "Granford is *dying!* There's nothing to bring people here any more. My parents can't sell bread to invisible people! And you standing there going 'But … but … but' like a stupid broken engine doesn't make any difference!"

And he stalked away furiously up the pavement, leaving Bella standing silent and hurt.

She felt stupid and angry. It wasn't as if she didn't *know* what was happening. She just hadn't wanted to believe it. And now Sam was treating her like an idiot. As if she didn't matter.

Well, if he was moving away then she *wouldn't* matter, would she? He'd find a new best friend at a new school.

Bella felt her insides boil and twist. She wouldn't run after Sam. No way. She turned left into Minerva Woods instead. There was a pretty woodland path that led around the back of the houses and eventually connected with the road where she lived. She wasn't meant to go this way on her own but she was too upset to care – or even notice. It seemed like her whole world was falling apart.

She ran along the path, pounding her feet hard on the damp pebbly surface, stamping her anger into the ground. Her backpack slapped up and down on her shoulder and a bit of homework from Mr Murphy slipped out of it. The worksheet, all about Romans in Britain, flew like a white bird into the bushes beside the path.

Bella came to a halt and let out a groan. She had to get it back. She had to do that homework tonight.

She dropped her bag on the path and began to pick her way through the bushes towards the sheet. It was caught in the branches of a holly tree. Trying to avoid the prickles, Bella reached in. But the paper suddenly curled in a gust of wind and flipped another three or four metres away towards a small clearing. With a shout of exasperation, Bella ran after it.

There was a weird noise. A kind of grating, groaning sound. Bella felt a rumbling beneath her feet.

And when she looked down at the ground, she discovered it wasn't there any more.

Bella screamed, teetering on the edge of a cliff which had appeared from nowhere. Sliding, scraping, popping noises filled the air along with the smell of earth and ripped up greenery. Bella gaped at the landslip beneath the toes of her shoes.

She could see mud and sticks and stones and leaves churning and tumbling. Birds flitted around in panic. She caught a white flicker of the Roman history worksheet in the stew of earth bubbling beneath her. And then there was nothing left to stand on and she dropped through thin air.

Chapter 4
Swallowed

For a long time Bella lay still, eyes screwed shut, not daring even to breathe. The thunderous noise settled down to creaks, rattles and gentle pings. Then silence. Was there still daylight above her? Yes. She could feel stuff on her legs and arms – cold and gritty – and a tickling across her cheek. Bella coughed, sneezed and opened her eyes. A long trailing stem of ivy was dangling in her face. Pebbles, earth, sticks and leaves lay in heaps across her – but when she struggled upwards on to her elbows, they fell away. She wasn't buried; just messy.

Carefully, she sat up in the pit. It was much deeper than the one she'd fallen into yesterday. There were no rusty iron cables in this one, just wriggling tree roots sticking out of the sides and some bits of old red clay.

It was wider too. You could easily fit a whole car into this one, like the big hole in town that she had seen on TV. The sides were steep but Bella thought she could probably climb out.

But what if the sides collapsed on top of her? Bella began to shake. No. She *had* to climb out.

Five minutes later she was still sitting, motionless, in the bottom of the hole. Despite the warmth of the day she was getting cold.

"Get *up*! Climb *out*!" she told herself, but she simply couldn't move. It was almost as if the ground had become a monster, opened its jaws and gulped her inside. Now it was sleeping again, with its mouth open. If she moved it might wake up and snap its teeth shut.

"BELLA! Beeeeee-llaaaaa!"

The voice ringing through the trees was Sam's. Bella finally managed to shake herself out of her shock.

"SAM! HELP! I'm down here!" she shrieked.

There was the sound of someone crashing through the trees above.

"Be careful! Don't fall!" she yelled up.

Sam's head appeared at the top of the hole. "Wow!" he said. "What are you doing down there?"

"Having a picnic!" snapped Bella. "What do you think?"

"Can you get out?" he called.

"I don't know." Bella tried to get up but felt a sudden stab of pain in her left ankle. She sank back again and shook her head. "My ankle really hurts."

"I'll come down," he said, cheerfully.

"No!" Bella shook her head. "Don't! If you get hurt we'll be trapped down here – and then what? You have to go for help."

"But I can climb down and—"

"—and make it all collapse even more!" yelled up Bella. "Sam, it's too dangerous."

"All right, all right!" said Sam. "But I don't like leaving you on your own."

"I'll be OK," she said, although she didn't feel OK. Her ankle was hurting more and more.

"I came to say sorry," he went on, holding on to a tree branch and leaning out to see her better. "For shouting at you. It's not your fault the town is dying. I shouldn't have been angry at you. I didn't expect you to run off and throw yourself over a cliff, though."

"Oh, ha ha!" said Bella, but she giggled. She was *so* glad Sam had come looking for her.

"This is freaky!" said Sam. "How many more of these are going to open up? Maybe Granford really will just slide into the earth!"

"Yeah – thanks for that thought!" said Bella with a shiver. "You'd better go."

"You sure you're OK, though?" he asked. "What does that ankle look like? Here!" He got a torch out of his backpack and chucked it down to her.

"You carry a *torch* in your bag?" she said, amazed.

"Yep. In case my best friend falls into a pit," he said, laughing.

Bella picked up the torch as it rolled towards her and switched it on. A quick look at her ankle showed that it was red and puffy. She prodded it and gasped with pain. "I think it's sprained," she said. "I can wriggle my toes, so it's probably not broken."

She shone the torch around her, into the darkness. And the darkness … glittered.

"What's this?" Bella picked up a small square of shining blue.

She dusted it off and it gleamed in her palm like a jewel. But it wasn't a jewel – the underside of it was some kind of clay.

"Throw it up to me," said Sam. Bella threw the square up and Sam caught it. It shone in his hand in a shaft of late afternoon sun.

"Here's another one. A yellow one. It's like … a tile," said Bella. "You know – those little tiles."

"Mosaic tiles," said Sam. "What else can you see?"

"More of the tiles – red and yellow and blue. And there are bits of red clay … like tubes. And some which are like flat squares."

Sam peered down. "Oh yeah – I can see them from here."

Some of the tubes poked up out of the rubble, firmly upright and had a square red tile on top. They seemed vaguely familiar to Bella as she ran her fingers over them.

Sam suddenly straightened up and looked excited. "Do you know what I think this is?" he said.

"Look, it doesn't matter. You really need to go and get help," said Bella.

"Yes – I will – but, Bella! This is amazing. I think you've found—"

But what Sam thought she'd found he didn't say. Because a moment later he had vanished.

Chapter 5
Petals and
Passages

"SAM!" Bella yelled, in panic. "SAM!" But all she heard – and *felt* – was more rumbling. The earth was shaking again and she screamed and put her hands over her head.

A few seconds later it was quiet once more, apart from a few pebbles rolling down the side of the pit. No more earth had dropped on her – but what had happened to Sam?

"SAM! Where are you?" yelled Bella, feeling a huge sob building up in her throat. There was no reply.

An angry magpie clacked in the branches above her and she could hear a distant aeroplane. But no Sam.

"I *told* you to go!" cried Bella. "I *told* you it wasn't safe! Why didn't you just do what I said?"

"Oh, do stop making such a fuss," said a voice, right behind her.

Bella shrieked and spun around, ignoring the pain in her ankle. Sam's face was peering out of a hole in the wall of earth and tree roots. It was covered in dirt but he was grinning. "You won't believe what I've just found," he said.

He fought his way through the roots and she saw that he was in a passageway. The little tiles she'd found in the pit around her must have come from the archway above his head. They were set into the walls and the ceiling of the passage, which was just high enough for Sam to stand up in. "What *is* this?" she murmured.

"Pass me the torch!" said Sam.

He shone the golden beam of light into the dark opening and at once the tiles gleamed back at them. They were arranged in a beautiful pattern of circles which overlapped each other, creating petal shapes.

There was a hole in the ceiling a short way in and daylight shafted through it, revealing bigger tiles on the floor. They were chalky white and not quite so shiny, but laid out in a style that made Bella think of fish scales.

"That's where I just fell through," said Sam, pointing to the hole. "The passage goes back the other way – deeper into the earth. There must be a room down there! An underground room!"

"It's beautiful!" Bella whispered, gazing at the mosaic.

Sam stood for a moment, peering into the passage. Then he groaned.

"What is it?" asked Bella.

"I *so* want to go and explore," he said.

"I know! So do I!" Bella wondered if she could hop inside the passage. She desperately wanted to find out where it went but her ankle was throbbing. She sighed and flopped back on her elbows. "Ouch!" Her arm had hit something hard. "What's that?"

Bella sat up again and carefully shifted around. Sam shone the torch next to her and then gave a low whistle. He gently pulled something out of the soil.

"It's a pot." Sam crouched down to stare at the pot. It was dark red with grooves around it. It stood as high as Sam's knee and had handles on the sides. Amazingly, it was in one piece.

"That's an urn," said Sam. "There's one on our homework worksheet."

Bella looked up. "Sam ... you don't think ... I mean, this couldn't be ...?"

Sam stared back at her. "I think it could be ..."

Bella tried to get up and then gave a little scream as her ankle burned. Sam turned away from the urn and looked at her.

"I can't believe I'm saying this, but we've got to forget about all this stuff. We've got to get you to hospital."

"You're having an attack of the sensibles!" said Bella, gently prodding her ankle and screwing her face up with pain. "Wow! Sam Williams is being *sensible!*"

Sam looked embarrassed and a little cross. "Look, I don't *want* to be sensible! I want to climb into that passage and find out what's inside! But it's too unstable. It's dangerous. And if I go in there and it falls on my head, who's going to get help for you?"

Bella smiled at him. "You'd better try to climb out then," she said. "I'll wait here."

Sam climbed up quite easily, using the tree roots as hand and foot holds. Bella could have done it too if her ankle wasn't hurt. Every time she moved it, pain shot up her leg and made her whimper.

"I'll be quick!" said Sam. "Don't worry." And he crashed away through the bushes. Soon there was no sound at all.

Bella took a deep breath and told herself to stay calm.

Chapter 6
Homework

Sam ran out of the woods and on to the road and then stood for a few seconds, wondering which way to go. Should he run to find Bella's parents? Or to the nearest house and ask to use the phone to call for the emergency services? And which emergency services did Bella need? Ambulance? Fire and Rescue? A helicopter?

He decided to run to Bella's house but the second he turned the corner he smacked into someone.

"Gah! Look out!" said the man, helping him up from the pavement. "Hey – Sam! Where are you off to?"

Sam was surprised to see it was Mr Murphy. "I … we … I mean … we've found something!" he blurted out.

"I see," Mr Murphy said, chuckling. "Something exciting? So exciting you're

running around out here rather than
sitting at the kitchen table, doing the
lovely homework I set for you!"

Sam thought for a moment, glancing at
the teacher's satchel. "Have you got another
one of those worksheets?" he asked.

"Why – have you lost yours?" Mr
Murphy said, pulling one out of the bag.

Sam took the worksheet and unfolded it, staring at the black and white drawings on it. His heart started beating fast. There was the picture of the urn. There was a picture of tiles in patterns like fish scales. There was even a picture of the red clay pipe things.

"Sir," he said. "About the homework … I've been doing some extra research with Bella. You might want to take a look."

"Well, I don't usually do that kind of thing outside school," said Mr Murphy, looking amused. "It's called *home*work for a reason, you know."

"Well, I *think* you might want to see this," Sam said. "Oh – and can you phone for an ambulance?"

Chapter 7
Rescue

Mr Murphy moved fast, calling for an ambulance on his mobile phone and running into the woods with Sam at the same time.

"BELLA!" yelled the teacher, batting springy branches out of his face. "We're on our way!"

Bella gave a shout back. She sounded all right.

Mr Murphy hurried to the edge of the pit. "Another sinkhole," he said. "This is getting out of hand." A metre from the edge he carefully leaned out to look down. "Bella! Are you OK?"

Bella peered up at him, pale and with earth in her hair. "Yes, I'm OK. My ankle hurts but I'm OK."

"The emergency services are coming," said Mr Murphy. "Bella, I'm not going to risk climbing down to you. I might cause more of a landslip. They're sending some cave rescue people who know all about this kind of thing."

"It's all right," said Sam. "I climbed up it all right. There are tree roots to hold on to." Sam reached for the roots to climb down but Mr Murphy grabbed his shoulder.

"No, Sam," he said. "Every time you go up or down the slope you're weakening it. We have to be patient and wait for the experts."

"Sir," called up Bella. "Look what we found." She held up the urn.

Mr Murphy's mouth fell open. He dropped to his hands and knees and peered down at the urn. Next to him, Sam held out the worksheet. "Is that what we think it is?" he asked.

"Well," said Mr Murphy, in a slightly cracked voice. "I can't be sure of course … but it really does *look* like a Roman urn."

"And what about these?" Bella shone the torch around the red clay pipes.

"Those," croaked Mr Murphy, "look very much like the pipes from a Roman bath house. My word. This is quite a find."

"There's a passageway too," called up Bella. "With mosaic tiles."

Mr Murphy almost squeaked. His eyes shone with excitement. "Well, I have to say, Sam and Bella, this is a first! No pupil I have ever taught has done their history homework quite like this!"

***

"HELLOOOO!" called a voice, a few minutes later, and Sam turned to see people coming through the trees. They wore boots and helmets with torches fixed to the front. They were carrying ropes, a stretcher and other equipment.

A woman reached them, followed by two men, all treading very carefully. "Step back now, please," she said. "We'll take over from here."

Bella beamed with relief. She was finally getting out of this hole. Then she looked around her and said, "Everyone – please climb down really carefully! There's treasure down here!" Her head swam as she watched her rescuers carefully shore up the side of the pit with wooden planks and a ladder. She was feeling very cold again.

She sank back down on to the earth and ran her fingers over the beautiful urn, keeping it safe as the first heavy boots landed beside her. "You're going to be just fine, Bella," said the woman in the helmet.

Bella smiled and then the woman and the pit and the urn faded away as she fainted.

Chapter 8
Hope in the Holes

"In total, seven sinkholes have appeared in Granford over the past three weeks," said the newsreader on national television. "And now – thanks to two schoolchildren and their teacher – we know why. It turns out that the town was built over an ancient Roman village, which archaeologists are now uncovering.

"It's thought to be the most complete Roman site ever found in this country – and we might never have found it if there hadn't been so much rain this year."

Bella's ankle had been badly sprained, but after a trip to hospital she'd been allowed to go home, bandaged up. Now, two weeks later, she could walk again.

Granford had never been busier. Bella and Sam were famous. So was Mr Murphy. They'd all been on TV and radio and in newspapers, talking about their adventure.

It was very exciting to watch all the experts arrive and start excavating the site. They were calling it Minerva Villa. Archaeologists had flown in from all over the world to study it. Teams of people were gently clearing all the tree roots and mud and stones out of the way and discovering more and more treasures, mosaics and wall paintings.

It turned out the other sinkholes were also over the remains of Roman buildings – but all the archaeologists were saying that none of the other houses were quite as beautiful and well preserved as Minerva Villa.

In Tasty Bakes, Sam's dad started making special Minerva Biscuits, shaped like Roman pots, and Minerva Buns with mosaic-style icing.

He couldn't make enough to keep up with demand. The town was buzzing with Bella and Sam's discovery. People just kept arriving: TV, radio and newspaper reporters, photographers, archaeologists and students.

Bella's mum and dad were trying out Roman hairstyles in the salon. They'd never had so many customers.

There were even new plans for the old factory. It was going to re-open as a Roman museum, displaying all the beautiful jugs, urns, plates and bits of jewellery that kept being found. This was just as well, because more and more tourists were arriving every day, fascinated by the buried Roman village.

In the weeks that followed, other shops re-opened. Brand new ones started up. Houses which had been left empty suddenly lost their shutters. Lights went on inside and overgrown gardens got tidied up. More children played in the park.

The school would definitely open again after the summer holidays. More and more families were arriving and their children would need to be taught.

Mr Murphy told them twenty-three new children were already on the register for next term. "And I'm not going anywhere," he said. "Granford is a history teacher's dream!"

But what made Bella the happiest was that Sam was staying. With Tasty Bakes now so busy, his dad didn't need to take the new job.

"So – things really *were* the pits," Sam said, as they walked to school past the brand new Minerva Villa Museum and Visitor Centre.

"Everything was going downhill," agreed Bella. "We were in such a hole."

"We had to hit rock bottom," went on Sam, laughing, "before things could get better."

Bella giggled and ran into the school

playground, spinning around. "Everything was nearly over for Granford!" she called back to Sam. "Then the Romans saved us all!"

"Watch out for the—" said Sam.

But Bella had already fallen into the sandpit.

"Not *again*," groaned Sam.

About the author

I've written more than 40 books for children. I live with my family in Southampton, England – on chalky soil! One year we'd had *so* much rain, I thought it might never stop. The roads were full of potholes and ruts – and then there were news reports of holes opening up and cars dropping right through them. I started to think about the land caving in and why it happens. And then I started wondering what might be hidden under the soil and grass and road surfaces. A sink hole would surely always be a disaster … wouldn't it?